POISON PAGES

BY MICHAEL DAHL
ILLUSTRATED BY MARTÍN BLANCO

Librarian Reviewer
Laurie K. Holland
Media Specialist (National Board Certified), Edina, MN
MA in Elementary Education, Minnesota State University, Mankato

Reading Consultant
Elizabeth Stedem
Educator/Consultant, Colorado Springs, CO
MA in Elementary Education, University of Denver, CO

 STONE ARCH BOOKS
Minneapolis   San Diego

Zone Books are published by Stone Arch Books,
151 Good Counsel Drive, P.O. Box 669,
Mankato, Minnesota 56002.
www.stonearchbooks.com

Copyright © 2007 by Stone Arch Books

Library of Congress Cataloging-in-Publication Data
Dahl, Michael.
    Poison Pages / by Michael Dahl; illustrated by Martín
Blanco.
    p. cm. — (Zone books - Library of Doom)
    Summary: When a girl starts reading a strange book
someone left on a bus, she suddenly finds herself inside its pages,
where the Librarian shows her how to avoid the poisonous letters
and other dangers.
    ISBN-13: 978-1-59889-327-4 (library binding)
    ISBN-10: 1-59889-327-0 (library binding)
    ISBN-13: 978-1-59889-422-6 (paperback)
    ISBN-10: 1-59889-422-6 (paperback)
    1. Books and reading—Fiction. 2. Librarians—Fiction.
3. Fantasy. I. Blanco, Martín, ill. II. Title.
PZ7.D15134Poi 2007
[Fic]—dc22   2006027534

Art Director: Heather Kindseth
Cover Graphic Designer: Brann Garvey
Interior Graphic Designer: Kay Fraser

1 2 3 4 5 6 12 11 10 09 08 07

Printed in the United States of America

TABLE OF CONTENTS

he Library of Doom is the world's largest collection of strange and dangerous books. The Librarian's duty is to keep the books from falling into the hands of those who would use them for evil purposes.

CHAPTER 1

THE EMPTY SEAT

The city is gray and cold. Rain falls from an angry sky.

A young girl holds an umbrella and waits for the bus to take her home.

The bus arrives full of sad, sleepy passengers.

The girl finds a place to sit, but there is a small, square shadow on the seat.

"Someone forgot their book," the girl says to herself.

She picks up the shadowy book and looks at the cover. Weird letters spell out `The Lost Readers`.

When she turns a page, the girl sees a picture of a gray girl waiting for a bus. The gray girl climbs onto a gray bus and finds a seat.

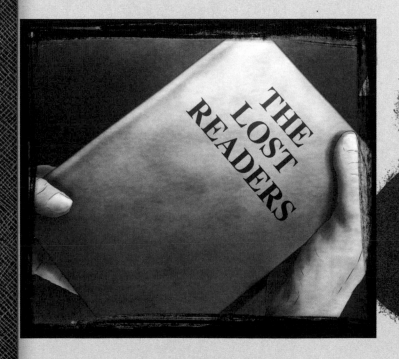

THE LOST READERS

On the next page is another picture. It shows the gray girl's seat, but this time the girl is gone.

Suddenly, on the real bus, the real girl is gone, too.

Only the **shadowy** book is left behind.

CHAPTER 2

THE ENDLESS FLOOR

The girl is no longer on the bus. She is outside. She is standing on a wide, flat floor. The floor is <u>endless</u>.

The endless floor is covered with black shapes.

She bends down and sees that the shapes are painted on the floor.

"Letters," says the girl.

"I am inside the book," she says to herself.

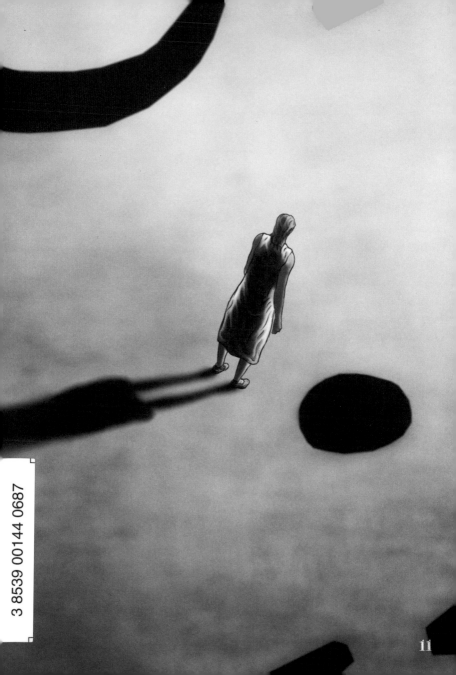

In the distance, the girl sees another shape. It is a man walking toward her.

The girl is frightened. She turns to walk away.

"Stop!" shouts the man. "Take one more step, and it will be your last!"

CHAPTER 3

THE LOST READERS

"Who are you?" asks the girl.

"I am the Librarian," says the man. "You have been taken by the book. Along with the others."

14

"Others?" says the girl.

The girl looks and now she can see other shapes.

Men, women, and children crowd around the `edges` of the endless floor.

15

"Who are they?" asks the girl.

"The lost readers," says the Librarian. "We are all inside the pages of the book."

The girl takes a step forward.

"I told you not to move," said the Librarian. "Do you want to end up like that?"

He points to a **figure** lying near them.

CHAPTER 4

A POISON PATH

The girl looks down. She was about to step on one of the <u>letters</u>.

"The letters are made of poison ink," says the Librarian.

"If you touch the poison, you will become part of the book forever."

"I've never heard of a poison book," says the girl.

"It is not an ordinary book," he says. "It comes from the Library of Doom."

"Follow me," he says. "Put your
feet where I put mine."

Carefully, they walk across the
endless floor.

"Let go!" the girl shouts.

One of the figures has grabbed her foot.

CHAPTER 5

TRAPPED ON THE PAGE

"Why?" gasps the figure. "Why?

The Librarian bends down and frees the girl's foot from the figure's grasp.

"He was poisoned by a question mark and cannot stop asking questions," says the Librarian.

The girl looks into the distance. She can see a faraway shape. It looks like a giant wave.

"The page is turning," says the Librarian.

The girl and the man race across the **vast floor**. ⟶

"Who are they?" asks the girl.

She sees some people tightly
wrapped with strips of paper.

They cannot move their arms or
legs. She hears them **moan**.

"Those are the library bound,"
says the Librarian.

"We cannot stop to help them."

The girl looks behind her. The
giant wave is **growing** closer.

❴ CHAPTER 6 ❵

OVER THE EDGE

The Librarian suddenly stops.

They are standing at the edge of the page.

Below them is a great darkness.

"You must jump," says the Librarian.

"But there's nothing there," the girl says.

"Trust me," says the Librarian.

The **giant** page is getting closer and closer.

"All right," says the girl.

She closes her eyes. She takes a
deep breath and jumps.

The **wind** rushes past her body.

Bump!

The girl opens her eyes. She is back on the bus.

She looks down at the book and sees a picture of the Librarian.

Why didn't he jump? the girl wonders.

At the bottom of the page she sees the words: There are more lost readers who **need my help**..

~ ◦ **THE END** ◦ ~

A PAGE FROM THE LIBRARY OF DOOM

LETTERS

Cambodia has the world's largest alphabet with 74 letters.

The world's shortest alphabet is used in the Solomon Islands of the South Pacific. It has only 11 letters.

Hawaiian is the next shortest with only 12 letters:

A E I O U H
K L M N P W

The most common letter in English is E.

W is the only letter in English that has more than one syllable.

In almost every language on Earth, the word for "mother" begins with the letter M.

ABOUT THE AUTHOR

Michael Dahl is the author of more than 100 books for children and young adults. He has twice won the AEP Distinguished Achievement Award for his nonfiction. His Finnegan Zwake mystery series was chosen by the Agatha Awards to be among the five best mystery books for children in 2002 and 2003. He collects books on poison and graveyards, and lives in a haunted house in Minneapolis, Minnesota.

ABOUT THE ILLUSTRATOR

Martín Blanco was born in Argentina and studied drawing and painting at the Fine Arts University of Buenos Aires. He is currently a freelance illustrator and lives in Barcelona, Spain where he is working on films and comic books. Blanco loves to read, especially thrillers and horror. He also enjoys soccer, the Barcelona football team, and playing the drums with his friends.

GLOSSARY

bound (BOWND)—trapped, tied up

grasp (GRASP)—to grab something firmly

seep (SEEP)—to flow slowly

vast (VAST)—very large

weird (WEERD)—strange

DISCUSSION QUESTIONS

1. At the end of the story, the girl is back on the bus. What do you think she should do with the book she found there? Why?

2. The Librarian is staying inside the book to help more lost readers. Do you think he will be able to rescue any more of them? Why or why not?

3. Sometimes people say they can "get lost" in a book. What do you think they mean by that?

WRITING PROMPTS

1. Imagine that you are trapped inside a book. It can be a real book that you have read, a comic book, or a book that you just made up. Write a story and describe what adventures you have. Are you able to escape?

2. What happens to the Librarian after the girl leaves? Who does he rescue next? What happens to him when the page turns? Write the next chapter in the Librarian's story.

INTERNET SITES

Do you want to know more about subjects related to this book? Or are you interested in learning about other topics? Then check out FactHound, a fun, easy way to find Internet sites.

Our investigative staff has already sniffed out great sites for you!

Here's how to use FactHound:

1. Visit *www.facthound.com*

2. Select your grade level.

3. To learn more about subjects related to this book, type in the book's ISBN number: **1598893270**.

4. Click the **Fetch It** button.

FactHound will fetch the best Internet sites for you!